Certain People

Certain People

& OTHER STORIES BY ROBERTA ALLEN

COFFEE HOUSE PRESS : : MINNEAPOLIS

Many of these stories have been published previously in the
following magazines: Appalachee Quarterly, Asylum,
Between C & D, Brix, Caprice, Central Park, Chelsea,
Continental Drifter, Fiction International, Helicon Nine,
Kalliope, and in the following anthologies: *Between C & D*
(Penguin), and *Border Lines* (Serpent's Tail)

Coffee House Press is supported in part by a grant provided
by the Minnesota State Arts Board, through an appropriation
by the Minnesota State Legislature, and by a grant from the
National Endowment for the Arts. Additional support has
been provided by the Lila Wallace-Reader's Digest Fund; The
McKnight Foundation; Lannan Foundation; Target Stores,
Dayton's, and Mervyn's by the Dayton Hudson Foundation;
General Mills Foundation; St. Paul Companies; Honeywell
Foundation; Star Tribune /Cowles Media Company; The
Butler Family Foundation; The James R. Thorpe Foun-
dation; and The Andrew W. Mellon Foundation.

Coffee House Press books are available to the trade through
our primary distributor, Consortium Book Sales & Distri-
bution, 1045 Westgate Drive, Saint Paul, MN 55114. For
personal orders, catalogs, or other information, write to:
Coffee House Press, 27 North Fourth Street, Suite 400,
Minneapolis, MN 55401.

Library of Congress CIP Data
Allen, Roberta,
    Certain people & other stories / Roberta Allen.
        p.   cm.
    ISBN 1-56689-052-7
    1. Manners and customs—Fiction.   I. Title
PS3551.L4157C4   1997
813'.54—dc20   96-17291
                                                        CIP

10 9 8 7 6 5 4 3 2 1

Contents

In memory of
Ann Bartur & John Fuggle
and
to David

House Hunting

In the neglected backyard of the run-down house, the man looks out of place. He glances disdainfully at goats grazing by the outhouse. He is agitated. He is distressed.

"Ninety thousand dollars for this dump!" he says to his companion, a woman from the States.

She stands by the back door watching him while a raven cries out from a gum tree. The cry sounds like a cry of distress. The cry sends a chill down her spine. The bird utters what the man feels, what the man cannot express.

The drab colors of dried-out weeds seem out of kilter with the bright Australian sky. Nothing fits, she thinks to herself.

Like a solid block the heat encloses them. The man mops his neck with a handkerchief. He is handsome, his casual clothes well cut.

A man like this would never buy this house. He is playing a game. He is killing time. It is Saturday afternoon. He likes to look at houses on Saturday afternoons and pretend that he might buy one. The woman knows he will not buy the house, but she humors him.

11

"I'd have to bulldoze the whole place," he says. "I'd have to start from scratch."

He already owns an expensive house in a wealthy suburb. He likes to pretend on Saturday afternoons that he will buy a cheaper place to live. He says he can't afford the mortgage now that his lover has left him. His lover, a beautiful American model, ran off with a cook. He can't believe that she left him for a cook!

The American woman standing by the door of the run-down house is not a model. She is not beautiful, but she is attractive. Before he met her, the man spent his free time alone.

"This house isn't so bad," she says. "At least it has character."

"Character! You call this character!" He points out the metal roof rusted from leaks. "Is that character? Do you think the yard has character too?"

The man is breaking down in the middle of the backyard, amidst weeds as dead as the garden he neglected in the yard of his expensive house.

The woman sees only his agitation. He walks back inside the house. He looks with disgust at the veils of dust, the unmade beds and dirty dishes, the strewn clothes and toys, the knickknacks and books scattered about.

The woman who owns the house is at work. The owner's husband left her, the real estate agent said. When the house is sold, the owner will move to the bush with her kids and raise goats.

"This is what a nervous breakdown looks like!" says the man, losing control. His eyes fill with tears. "This is what happens when a lover is betrayed!"

The man moves away when the woman tries to console him. The man understands the way the owner feels better than he understands the woman who is with him.

He can't understand what a woman could see in a man who was left for a cook! He likes the *idea* that a woman is there, but he can't focus on her face. He can't admit that he likes to have her with him. He can't see that maybe, sometime in the future, he might want this woman by his side. To him, the way it is now is the way it will always be.

The man knows he is breaking down, but he doesn't know what breaking down is. He uses words, but he no longer is sure that they mean what he thinks they mean. There is so much space between what he feels and what he says he feels. Sometimes he doesn't know any words to describe how he feels, though he went to Oxford.

The woman is good with words. Sometimes she finds better words than he can to describe what he feels. Sometimes words come pouring out of him that she catches in her hands. She holds them lovingly, turns them around to see them from all angles. He is afraid to admit that he likes the woman for doing that. For cradling his words. For handling them gently. He can't give her anything but words. Everything else is stopped up.

Everything else he's buried deep inside, in a place that he can't see, because he's too afraid to see. He wanders through the rooms like a ghost. He's afraid that if he sees, everything will come pouring out. Then she'll really see who he is. Then he'll have nothing left. He no longer sees the house. The sloping floors, the peeling walls are pictures of himself. He closes his eyes.

Perhaps she would handle him the way she handles his words. In a way, he would like her to handle him the way she handles his words, but he no longer trusts the word "lovingly." He slides his fingers over a dusty bookcase. He needs to touch something.

He can't let himself be handled again except if he can't help it. He's afraid he won't be able to help it. He's afraid he'll pour like water into the woman's hands. Then he will be lost. He laughs. He is already lost in a yard filled with weeds, in a house full of dust and dirty dishes, in an unmade bed with crumpled sheets. He is lost on the termite-eaten veranda where he stands, and behind the wheel of his car. His mail lies on the backseat, unopened for a week.

There is a great empty space where he used to be. He tries to fill that space with words. His words. Her words. It doesn't matter. He sees that empty space in every house, in every face where he's removed the features.

He looks at his watch. There are so many houses to see. There are so many houses he never will buy. If he could release himself, he could move. He wouldn't be stuck. He could buy a house. He could take flight. He could leave the lover who left him. He could avoid his own blows. But his own fist flies in his face, and he is powerless to duck the punch. The woman would like to push him out of his way, but she is smart enough to know better. She knows he will take away his words if she makes one false move.

The Pear

The pear lies in a red bowl in the bald man's study.
The pear is rotting; its flesh is soft and mottled.
The bald man forgot he put the pear in the red
bowl; he just wanted to fill the bowl the same way
he filled the house: ornate mirrors reflect a profu-
sion of plants, pre-Colombian figures, and por-
traits of his children now grown; the library
overflows with books and periodicals stacked from
floor to ceiling. The bald man sits on the sofa in the
living room staring into space. A large picture window faces him. He doesn't see the blue sky or the
trees or the low-flying planes in formation. All he
sees is his wife, who has left him. Cartons filled
with her belongings stand piled behind the sofa
where the bald man cannot see them. His face
looks ashen. Even his mustache seems drained of
color. Blue veins like the tributaries of a river on a
map glisten on his smooth skull. On the open
book in his study, his patients' names are still read-
able beneath the red scrawled "canceled" across the
page. Though there is a fresh white cloth on the
headrest of his couch, no patients rest their heads
here today; no tales of turmoil pass from their lips.

Toward nightfall, as pinks and mauves flush the sky and a rosy tint colors the rooms, the maid enters with a key. Without a sound she slips inside the kitchen. She cooks his evening meal, which he eats in silence. The maid dusts the other rooms. Seeing the rotting pear in the red bowl, she throws it in the trash. The next day the bald man notices the empty bowl. He thinks about the pear, desiring it now that he can no longer have it, the same way he desires his wife.

Tarantula

I'm not looking at the tarantula. I'm looking at him, as he examines the stones in the wall of this great Mayan ruin. Everyone else is examining the dead tarantula I found on the temple platform. The spider, as big as my hand, has sharp black hairs on its abdomen that sting when the creature is alive. I have seen tarantulas before. But I have never seen my companion act so distant. The people in this group think we are strangers. No one here would suspect we have a past. They think we just met at the guest house this morning where this trip to the ruins began. Every crypt, every altar, every Mayan mound covered with trees and vines excites him. The excitement he felt for me he has transferred to Mayan stones. He touches them lovingly. Like a dancer he leaps across them, caressing them lightly with his feet. As he grows light, I grow heavy. As heavy as the Mayan stones. I feel my skin turn hard and gray and rough. I am rain-soaked, battered by winds, beaten by sun. Ants crawl over me. Birds leave their droppings. But the group sees only the tarantula, which is beginning to decompose.

The Cockroach

The cockroach on the wall is enormous. If I were alone here, I would take out the repellent in my duffel and spray the cockroach dead. Instead, because he is here, I am acting like "the girl." I am making faces to show my revulsion. He is responding like "The Knight In Shining Armor." "My Hero" is swatting the cockroach with a shoe. I'm only glad he's not using his hands. He's obsessed with killing flies and mosquitoes, which he squishes between his fingers. Later, when he touches me, I try to forget about the insects that he's killed. There's no sink in this room to wash our hands. There's no water. When we bathe in the field where the cows graze, in a three-walled shed of corrugated zinc, we carry pails of rainwater from the vat by the police station down the road. At night we protect ourselves from flies and mosquitoes with a sheet. Our arms and legs are wrapped around each other despite the unbelievable heat. We are melting into one another. We are dissolving: nothing can stop us, except perhaps a sudden cold spell.

Spoiled

Sand stings her eyes, whips her skin. Will it ever let up? she wonders, shielding her eyes with her hand. No place to run for cover, the girl and the man huddle beneath the beach blanket. Mercilessly the sand assaults them on the unspoiled beach. Nothing but sand blowing for miles around. The man and the girl wish there was a boat, wish there was a way to escape the sand. So mysterious that the sea is calm, yet how this sand blows! Not a living thing can be seen, not even a bird. The beach blanket is no protection. They cannot pretend this is a fine day at the beach. Nothing is fine between them. The girl sees the man through a haze of sand. The sand is like a fine screen between them. He is vague, his voice muffled, his motions slowed by the whirling drifting sand. Together, arm in arm, carrying the wine, the bread and cheese, the towels, and the beach blanket, they fight their way through the merciless sand, heads bowed, eyes squinting. This picnic on the perfect beach spoiled by sand. This picnic spoiled before it took place, long before it happened. This picnic spoiled by the man's infidelity months before. Sand couldn't spoil this picnic, she sees clearly for the first time in months.

The Fly

There's a fly in my ear. I hear it buzzing. It can't get out. It's not the only insect I hear buzzing. There are plenty of biting flies and mosquitoes in this tiny room, but fortunately, the others are not in my ear. The flies and mosquitoes come in through the open windows. We have to keep the windows open, otherwise we would die from the heat. I wake him up. There's a fly in my ear, I tell him at 3 A.M. He turns on the flashlight, takes a pair of tweezers from a case. Carefully, he extracts the insect, shows it to me. It's bigger than I thought. He goes back to sleep. But I stay awake, thinking about this fly in my ear. What would I have done if he wasn't here? Somehow that seems to be the wrong question. I have traveled all over the world. Never before have I had a fly in my ear. Why now? If I was alone, surely this wouldn't have happened. This happened only because he is here. This romance has made my head spin. I have let myself get carried away. Maybe that fly was trying to tell me something. Maybe that fly was trying to bring me back to earth. Do I sound absurd? Did that fly mean nothing at all? Is meaning only something we add on to things?

The Pain is Coming

In the backyard of the house in Perth where the woman stays, there is a lovely garden where she can pick fresh figs for breakfast. Grapevines grow by the door. The shadiest part of the garden is as dark and tangled as a forest. Kookaburras and parrots, galahs and blue-breasted wrens chatter in the trees. A mesh cage with canaries stands in the shade of the big red gum. At night the caretaker covers the cage with a cloth.

The man knows the names of all the plants and shrubs, trees and vines in the garden. He tests the limes, the pomegranates to see which fruits are ripe. The woman collects fallen eucalyptus pods from the red gum tree. They are large and swollen. They feel like something prehistoric in her hand.

The man and the woman lie in the shade of the gum tree on chaise lounges. The man will take his vacation soon, he says.

"Where will you go?" asks the woman.

"Down south to Margaret River, where I spent my summers when I was a child. I want to recapture the happiness of my youth," he says, with a sigh.

The woman feels like shaking him. Wake up! she wants to cry. Look around you! But she says nothing. She is happy lying in the shade of the big red gum. She is happy because the man is beside her.

The man is happy too, but he doesn't know it. The only way he can be happy is by hiding his happiness from himself. This is a game he plays. He has learned a trick. He has learned to steal a little happiness when he isn't looking.

What is he thinking about as he lies there looking so relaxed? He isn't thinking about anything. He is letting his mind drift with the fragrant odors in the air. He is letting the sounds of birds and the woman's voice soothe him. He is hearing the swish of leaves in the trees overhead. He is sipping cool liquid in a glass.

A smile starts on his face, but he stops himself. Like an open door his face slams shut. He feels ashamed. He feels embarrassed. He feels as though he's caught himself with his pants down. He's not supposed to be happy. Has he forgotten that his lover left him for a cook?

How did he manage to escape himself? It must be the woman's fault. It was she who made him forget. It was she who lulled him with her voice. It was she who invited him into the garden, but he didn't have to go.

The woman is aware of his smile that almost happened. She thinks it's a shame that he won't allow himself to have his happiness. Even his happiness he pushes away. Did he push away his lover? she wonders.

The man has a wry ironic sense of humor when he lets himself have anything. He laughs despite himself. It is easier to laugh than to smile. He laughs to hide his embarrassment. After all, the woman almost saw him happy. He erases almost everything she saw with his ironic sense of humor. "You are so cynical," she sighs.

The caretaker, a woman from South Africa, watches them from the upstairs window. She has nothing better to do, and this is quite a good show. The man is so handsome. She wonders if they will fall in love. How can a woman resist a man who is so handsome!

The caretaker reveres beauty. She knows all about being beautiful. When she was young, she was beautiful. One can still see traces of her beauty. Her skin is translucent, her features small and fine. Her white hair is as soft as babies' hair.

Early in the morning when she waters the garden, she wears long nightgowns as translucent as her skin. Only her head, covered in a large sun hat, is hidden from view. One would not be surprised to see such a diaphanous figure dissolve in the air. One would not be surprised to find only her hat among the pale pink boronias.

The man knows that the woman is going to a party tonight with another man. She told him so before they made the date this afternoon. He is relieved to know she has another date: he feels less pressured now.

It is beautiful lying in the garden. He feels as though he never wants to leave. The more he knows he should leave, the harder it is for him to rouse himself. He feels as though he is under a spell. Perhaps she has cast a spell over him.

He drifts back into the forbidden happiness he allowed himself so briefly. Now he smiles easily. His smile is warm. When the woman sees him smile, she knows why she likes to be near him.

When the light dims, the mosquitoes come out. The couple go inside. The man opens the piano she has never used. He plays popular tunes. She is surprised to see him so animated. Is it happiness or desperation that enlivens him?

He is playing the piano to delay the pain because he knows the pain is coming. He knows his happiness will soon end. He is trying to keep his mind off his happiness. If he thinks about his happiness, he will have to think about the pain. When he is playing the piano, he doesn't have to think. He is just playing, but he knows the pain is coming even while he is playing. Even when he isn't thinking, he knows the pain is coming. Because he knows the pain is coming, he is no longer happy. He is playing faster and faster. His fingers are banging the keys.

The doorbell rings. The moment he dreaded has arrived. His face falls like a curtain onstage. He closes the piano.

As he leaves, he says good-bye in a stiff formal manner. There is pain on his face, but he tries not to show it. He looks so lost the woman kisses him.

The woman and her date watch his car drive crazily ahead of them. He is trying to shake off the pain. He is trying to lose it, outsmart it. He is driving like a madman, swerving from side to side on the road, imprisoned by his pain like a fly in a block of ice. He tries to break through any way he can.

He is feeling the pain on all sides. He is driving straight into the pain. He is speeding home to the empty house where his lover left him for a cook. He slows down. He knows now why he stops himself from being happy. There is no pain worse than the pain he feels after being happy.

The woman watches his car pull into a gas station. She feels so sorry. He is all alone. Is anyone more alone?

The caretaker has witnessed both departures through the upstairs window. She wonders why the man left alone and why the woman left with someone else. If I were her, she sighs, I wouldn't let him get away. She won't find another like him.

I Am Beautiful?

Is he crazy? Must a man be crazy to leap from a cafe across the street to tell me I am beautiful? He is saying I am beautiful. This handsome man with a tan and a body that surpasses the ideal. A little while ago, I was looking at my picture in the newspaper. There was my picture on page fifteen. I was thinking how old, how tired, how unattractive I look. Now suddenly this handsome man—much younger than me—appears out of nowhere to tell me I am beautiful! Is this a joke? A terrible joke?

"Have a drink with me," he is saying. But he can't stand still. He is jogging in place. Why is he so nervous? He is begging me to have a drink with him.

"Who are you?" I ask in the restaurant. "Tell me something I can believe."

"I am a scaffolder from Sydney," he says. "I live across the street."

"What do you want from me?" I ask him. I want this to be more than a joke.

"You are beautiful," he says again.

I tell him I am hungry. I want to have dinner. He says he'll stay if I let him, he'll leave if I tell him to go.

"Tell me more about yourself," I say. But he can't

sit still. His eyes dart, his hands fidget, he starts speaking in rhymes. When the manager eyes us suspiciously, I say, "I think you better go."

At the door, he turns the Open sign around to Closed, and gives me one last look.

Earthly Pleasures

After the opening of her gallery exhibit in New York, the well-known Italian sculptor with a Cleopatra hairdo drives with her dealer and his wife to their large uptown duplex, tastefully furnished with expensive paintings and antiques. A number of distinguished guests soon arrive. The artist feels exhausted; for several nights she's lain awake in her hotel. Preoccupied with her show, she barely notices the city. She should feel happy, she tells herself, as she sits in an overstuffed chair greeting guests. Her English is as minimal as her sculptures inspired by ancient Egyptian art. A maid serves rounds of champagne on a tray. But the Italian woman wishes she was home. Two maids serve a lavish seafood dinner in her honor in a lofty candlelit dining room. Facing her at the table sits a well-known painter, once her lover, with his young wife. The Italian woman, her sad eyes staring into space, suddenly begins to cry. Everyone discretely looks away. Her former lover hides his face with a napkin as he dabs his mouth, while his embarrassed wife stares at her full plate. The artist, who has no appetite, feels a terrible sense of loss; the work that absorbed her for a year is finished; the opening she anxiously awaited is past. The taste of vintage wine, the sight of snapper and bass, salmon and caviar, lobster and mushrooms, fail to stir her senses. The guests raise their glasses in a toast, but she sees their faces blur as tears smear her mascara and roll down her cheeks. She suddenly remembers an ancient Egyptian custom at banquets: in order to stimulate the guests to enjoy earthly pleasures to the full, a coffin was sometimes brought in containing an imitation skeleton so that they would appreciate more highly the good things of life, especially those of the table. As she recalls this image, she suddenly laughs out loud. The guests look in her direction, surprised. Embarrassed, she lowers her eyes but raises her fork to eat the sumptuous dinner on her plate.

The Flat

The publisher of the art magazine doesn't act like other married men in Australia. He buys me lunch. He opens the car door for me. He's Italian. As we pass in the car, he points out the flat he just rented. He says he rented the flat because he needs to be alone two nights a week. I glance at the flat. He gives me a look. It's not the kind of look married men usually give me, unless they want to fool around. But maybe he's just trying out the look. Maybe he just wants to see how it feels. He looks like a man who feels as though he can do anything he wants. I think he wants to invite me to his flat. Having the flat gives him the choice of inviting me or not. He would probably want to invite me to his flat more if he didn't have one. Maybe he has the flat so he won't invite me. Maybe having the flat is a test. Maybe he is like a smoker who has given up cigarettes, but keeps a pack around just to know he can smoke if he chooses. I am thinking about the look and I am thinking about his wife and child. I have a choice too.

Drawing

In her studio at the museum, she is drawing, always drawing. She can figure things out when she is drawing. She can talk to herself in a language without words. A language of lines and forms and colors. Drawing is her secret language. People like her drawings, but no one sees her drawings the way she sees them. They are parts of herself. When she looks at her drawings, she sees the secrets that only she knows.

The museum in Australia liked her drawings well enough to fly her here from the States. This is a boring place. All the movie theaters show the same three films.

Maybe she wouldn't think about the man so much if she had something else to do when she's not drawing. When she's drawing she's not bored, but when she stops for the day, she has only the man to think about. Even when she is drawing the man is not far away. He is there in the drawings. No one else can see him in the circles, the squares, the swirling lines, but he is there.

Wherever she is, the room where she works is her world. How easily she leaves her world when he calls and invites her to lunch. She is astonished at how easy it is to throw her work aside. As though it means nothing. As though she was only killing time. Her studio is nothing but a room now, which she is trying to leave quickly. She can hardly believe she can throw aside her work so easily to run and meet a man!

He is waiting by the desk in the museum lobby. How small he looks from a distance. How insignificant. Is it worth leaving her work to run and meet this man? This man whose lover left him for a cook. Perhaps he will never recover. Perhaps she is wasting her time. Why can't she see that she might be wasting her time?

He is relieved when he sees her. "I must look terrible," he says, apologetically. "I should have changed my clothes."

"You look fine," she says, taking his arm. But he doesn't look fine. She's never seen him like this. He's so pale. So fragile. He's shaking.

"I took the day off from work," he says. "I read all morning in the library. I like reading history. It takes me out of myself. I can pretend to live in another time."

They go to a pub nearby. The woman is greeted by the assistant curator, who is young and handsome.

"Who was that?" he asks, anxiously.

"Just a guy who works at the museum."

"Just a guy," he echoes, looking uncertain. He wishes he had shaved. He wishes he was wearing his three-piece suit.

They drink beer at a table outside.

"I had a terrible weekend," he says. "The worst weekend I ever had. I stayed alone in my family's house in Margaret River. My parents were so frightened when I called, they drove down in a panic. Mother thinks I have a chemical imbalance. She wants me to see a psychiatrist."

"I think that's a good idea," says the woman.

"Of course you would. You're American! But Australians don't see psychiatrists unless they've gone bonkers." He pauses. "Maybe I should see one. For two days I couldn't get out of bed. I lay there trying to find a reason, any reason at all, to get out of bed. There seemed to be no point to living."

"And now?"

"I'm a little better. At Margaret River, Mother held me, stroked me the way she did when I was a child. I needed to be held. I needed to be stroked. I couldn't stop crying."

He looks around the cafe, nestled in the shade between two buildings. "There is something missing in this city," he says. "Something is wrong here."

"There's no soul," says the woman. "All that matters here is money. If the museum hadn't given me this fellowship, I wouldn't stay."

"I thought I was satisfied here," says the man. "I enjoyed making money. I used to like my life."

Listening to his own voice, the man has the sensation that someone else is speaking. Is this his voice? Even touching his arm is a strange sensation. Is this his arm? Is *he* touching his arm? Who is here in place of him? Has he performed the ultimate magician's trick? Has he disappeared from himself? There must be a trace. A clue. But he has nothing to go on. He is a missing person. He is a mystery he cannot solve. He needs to speak. He needs to hear his voice even if it isn't his voice.

"I want to find myself," he says. "I want to find something that has meaning."

"Why don't you come to my studio?"

"Now?" he asks, looking unsure. "You know I won't understand your work."

"Come anyway," she says, smiling.

He wonders if he knows the woman at all as he walks around the large light room. The lines and forms and colors in her drawings on the wall look to him like a kind of hieroglyphics that only an expert can decode.

"At least you have a world of your own," he says, "that isn't dependent on others."

"I couldn't live without my world," the woman says.

He tries to find some trace of the woman he knows in the drawings. But the drawings are a mystery to him. The woman is a mystery to him, because she made the drawings.

There are so many layers in a human life, layers he doesn't see. He tries to see because he knows there is so much he doesn't know how to see. Perhaps if he knew how. Perhaps if she would teach him.

He looks at the large table where she works. Is that cardboard covering the surface? Cardboard, stained and warped and soaked with color, bleeding. As though a battle had been fought. A battle he can't imagine, though he knows about battles. Battles with himself. Is this the scene of her battles?

What are the little bits of things lying like casualties on the bloody cardboard? He goes closer. Little sticks of color. Little boxes like open coffins. Pencil shavings. Razor blades. Pen points. Brushes. Jars of color. Scraps of paper. Pieces of cloth like bloody bandages ripped from wounds. Battle dust hangs in the air.

This is a table where something happens. How does she make something happen on this motley table with these humble tools? This is a table full of secrets. Teach me, he wants to say.

He turns to look once more at the drawings. He never thought before of circles and squares and swirling lines emerging from a battle.

The woman smiles as she watches him. She smiles because she knows he is there in those drawings, though he cannot see himself. He is there in those circles and squares and swirling lines. He is there in those shadows, in those spaces. He is there in her world without knowing. Without knowing, he is there.

The Visitor

In New York, the plump German painter exhausts her American friends with her enthusiasm; everything excites her, inspires her. Though she pays exorbitant rent and sleeps on a mattress on the floor of the run-down studio in the Bowery where she paints, nothing bothers her but the thought of going home: her money will not last long here.

One morning she receives an unexpected call from the German dealer who shows her work at home. "Uta, what are you doing here?" the painter asks, surprised.

"I felt like getting away. In your letters you sounded so ecstatic about New York, I wanted to see for myself. Is your invitation still open?" she asks, coyly.

The painter suddenly remembers saying in a letter that she was welcome to stay in her loft if ever she came to New York. She never imagined Uta would take her offer seriously. "Of course," she replies, as she wonders what to do.

"Can I come now?" Uta asks. "I'm at the airport. I'll take a taxi."

"Sure," the painter says, growing anxious. So this

43

is how Uta expects to save money, she tells herself. Imagine, Uta with her fussy habits staying here! She shakes her head as she pictures Uta with her mania for cleanliness, washing ashtrays after every smoke. She sees Uta, pampered by her maid and wealthy husband, guzzling wine at openings when no one sees, then flirting with every man in sight. As she glances round the room, she knows it's hopeless to clean; she doesn't even put her scattered clothes back in the suitcase on the floor, where she keeps them.

Wearing work clothes, the painter answers the door. Uta looks nervous, her fuchsia lipstick bleeds beyond her lipline. Strands of platinum hair stick to her forehead in the heat. She wobbles on high heels. Her dress is creased. "Oh, I need to lie down!" Uta says. Her fingers touch her aching head. "Such heat! Such filth! So many people!"

The painter leads her inside. Uta's blue eyes widen. "Here? You expect me to stay here?" Uta shrieks. "You are living like an animal! Who would believe you were once a doctor's wife! You never lived like this at home!"

"Here I feel free!" the painter says, angrily.

In the room, beside the mattress, stand several large unfinished canvases, an easel, a chair, and a stool. Small paintings and drawings hang on one wall. Discarded paper lies crushed in a corner. Uta stares at the walls, their rotting wooden slats exposed. She stares at cracked windowpanes, at warped floorboards stained with color, at the paint-smeared sink, at the makeshift shelves, which hold jars of paint, brushes, and tubes of color.

"Where do you cook?" Uta asks, ignoring the paintings.

"I don't cook. To save money, I eat peanuts for dinner." After a pause she adds defensively, "Peanuts are healthy!"

Uta powders her nose, and breathes deeply to calm herself. "Well, I can't stay here," she says, while studying her face in her compact mirror. "Can you find me a hotel—not too expensive?" she asks. The painter, barely concealing her rage, reluctantly opens a phone book. She had forgotten the contemptuous way Uta had always treated her at home. She had forgotten Uta's power to hurt her. In New York everything was so different! The painter sends her off to a midtown hotel in a taxi.

Alone in her loft the painter wonders why she let her come. As she sits there brooding, she looks out the large dirty windows at the city: for the first time New York feels like home.

Brief Encounters

This is not the sort of bar where one expects to find the commercial counselor of the Bulgarian Embassy. With his handlebar mustache, he looks as though he stepped out of the nineteenth century.

"I want to order something very American. What would you suggest?" he says, with a strong accent.

"How about Jack Daniels?" I reply.

"What's that?"

"Bourbon."

"Alright," he says, smiling.

"How would you like it?" I ask.

"Oh, any way the Americans drink it," he says.

"Well, do you want ice, soda, or water?"

"Anything you want to give me will be fine," he says.

Someone has played a song by Prince on the jukebox. The Bulgarian nods his head in time to the beat. "This is a place to see a slice of New York life," he says, glancing down the bar at the construction crew—my regular customers—who are arguing over a Mets game.

"How long have you been here?" I ask.

"Two years," he says, "but soon I will go back to Bulgaria for a new assignment. I lived in Argentina before I came here. I've lived in many countries."

"What does a commercial counselor do?" I ask.

"I sell Bulgarian products to foreign companies. Everyone thinks Bulgaria is a backward nation—and in many ways it is: we are still largely agricultural, but we make very good tractors, for example, that we sell very cheap."

"It must be hard moving from place to place," I say.

"No, I enjoy living in different countries. But it's harder for my wife. She doesn't like to move around so much, especially now that we have a little daughter. Are you French?"

"No."

"You look French. I could swear you are French."

"I'm not."

Narrowing his eyes as if to see me better, he says, "You don't seem quite at ease."

"Well, I'm new at this," I reply.

"It shows," he says, smiling, "but I think you're charming."

"Thank you."

The word "charming" sounds strange here.

The Bulgarian keeps glancing at a picture of the Beatles, screen-printed on a mirror hanging over the bar.

"I like that picture. I really like that picture! Could I buy it?" he asks.

"I'm not the owner. You'd have to ask him," I say.

Mr. M., my boss, has something for every taste in this bar.

"I really want that picture. That is America to me! That would be the perfect memento to bring back to Bulgaria!"

"Well, he usually calls late in the afternoon. I can ask him for you."

I wonder if he knows the Beatles are English.

A young Scottish waiter from a nearby restaurant sits down beside him.

"How are you today?" I ask.

"Could be better," he says. "Last night I lost a big tip. This group of women came in and drank away their money before they ordered dinner. They didn't know the restaurant doesn't take credit cards."

The Bulgarian looks at him. I don't think he's met many off-duty waiters in New York.

"The restaurant is nearby?" he asks, in a friendly way.

"Just two blocks over on Second." He turns to me, "I'll have a Jack on the rocks."

"Did you order Jack Daniels?" asks the Bulgarian.

The waiter nods.

"That's what I'm drinking too. Very American, hmm?"

"I guess so," the waiter says.

"Where do you come from?" asks the Bulgarian.

"Glascow, but I worked my way through France and Germany before I came here."

"Oh," says the Bulgarian. "So you know something of Europe. Let me buy your drink."

"Cheers!" says the waiter, lifting his glass.

A heavy red-haired woman sits down a few seats away.

"Oh, I need something strong," she says, with an accent. "I'll have a scotch and soda." She looks around the bar. "I've passed this place a thousand times, but I've never been inside. It doesn't look so bad," she says, surprised. "I rarely drink in the afternoon, but I'm so upset today! Do you have children?"

"No."

"Well, I wish I never had! The way my daughter treated me this afternoon makes me sorry I ever gave birth! Imagine having a daughter who walks several paces behind you on the street because she's ashamed that you're her mother! She's too good for me now—a stockbroker!

"We argued on the street over where to have lunch. We couldn't go where anyone might know her—she didn't say that but that's what she meant—so I walked off without saying a word and left her standing on Fifth Avenue. But I feel terrible! What should I do?"

"Talk to her," I say.

"She'll deny everything, say it's all in my head, but I'm no fool."

"I think you should try," I say. "I'm sure she's upset too."

She says with a sigh, "You're probably right."

I serve more beer to the construction crew, who

are laughing like schoolgirls at the other end of the bar, and bring another round to the Bulgarian and the waiter, who seem to have a lot to say to one another.

"I could still swear you are French," the Bulgarian says to me.

"I'm no more French than I was half an hour ago," I reply.

The Bulgarian laughs. I think the Jack Daniels is going to his head. "Let me have a beer too," he says, glancing at the construction crew, still in high spirits. Two of them are having a mock fight while the others cheer them on.

The red-haired woman looks over at the Bulgarian. "Do you have children?" she asks.

"Yes, I have a daughter, three years old," he says.

"Mine is twenty-eight, a stockbroker. She was born here, but I'm from Egypt, and so was her father. I guess that's not the right background for a stockbroker. She should have socialite parents on Park Avenue, I suppose. I bet she doesn't tell her friends that her mother's a registered nurse from Egypt."

The Bulgarian looks impatient. "Egypt! Bulgaria! Scotland!" he says, waving his hands in the air. "What difference does it make? Everyone here comes from someplace else. That's what makes this city so interesting," he says, smiling at the woman.

She looks sorry that she spoke.

The Bulgarian is drinking at a faster and faster

pace. I pour less Jack in his drinks, but it doesn't seem to help.

"This is a pleasant place to spend the afternoon," he says to me, cheerfully, but his words are slurred.

The woman drinks two more rounds, and leaves a large tip on the bar. "I feel better," she says to me, rising from her seat. "I'm going to call my daughter when I go home, and get everything off my chest. I was afraid to tell her how I feel, but now I have more courage. I'll let you know how it went," she says, smiling.

When the waiter gets up to leave, the Bulgarian looks at his watch, surprised. "I never imagined it was this late!"

He takes a last look at the picture of the Beatles as he rises, gripping the bar for support. "I still want that picture," he says. "I'll have to come back soon."

"Don't worry. I won't let anyone else buy it," I say, as he staggers toward the door. I'm sure he won't be back. I wonder whether I'll see the woman from Egypt again, but my thoughts are interrupted by the sudden laughter of the construction crew, who are ready for another round of beers.

A Hole in Her Memory

Tara is not yet ready to go home to Ireland. But she is getting ready. She is almost ready. Every day she is a little more ready. There's nothing much to keep her in Australia now. There's nothing much left for her to do. Still, it's hard for her to leave Australia. She's been living here for almost a year. A year is a long time in the life of someone twenty-six. A year can feel like a lifetime.

Tara runs a little gallery in Ireland. She tried to sell the work of her young artists here. Their paintings didn't sell. She almost sold a painting called *The Outhouse*. But when she saw it on a rich collector's bathroom door, she grabbed it back, saying, "In Ireland, an outhouse is a farmhouse!"

Tara is disappointed. Her artists will be disappointed when she tells them that their paintings didn't sell. Tara is getting ready to tell them. Tara is getting ready to go home.

Tara is getting ready to go home, but she's not quite ready. She's too hungover to think of going home today. Tara learned to drink in Australia. She learned to drink with the curator, a gay man, who lives next door.

Very little scares Tara. But Tara is scared now. She is standing in the shower, staring at her thighs in disbelief. There are bruises on her thighs! She is staring at her thighs as though they belong to someone else. She is scared because there is a hole in her memory.

A million things are running through her mind. She wants to say STOP to her mind, but she knows it wouldn't do her any good, as she looks at her body—her body which is not her body.

Stepping out of the shower, she wishes she was home. Home in her mother's house in Ireland. If she was home in her mother's house in Ireland, she wouldn't have bruises on her thighs. Her thighs would look the way they've always looked. A little plump perhaps, but creamy and smooth.

She is brushing her teeth and looking in the mirror at a woman she doesn't know. How could she know a woman with bruises on her thighs? She is splashing water on her face. While splashing water on her face, she doesn't have to see this woman she doesn't know.

She has seen enough of this body that isn't her body. Now she is looking at her mind. Among the million things running through her mind, she sees fragments from last night. She is clearing a space among the million things so she can focus on the fragments and fit them together.

In the picture forming in her mind, she sees herself and the curator at the museum, attending an opening. The room looks dark in her memory, long and dark, more like a passage than a room.

She sees many faces, hears the sound of clinking glasses. Champagne. The champagne glows like pale gold. Pale gold flows into the glasses. Tara feels the pale gold sliding down her throat. The room is dim but glowing with champagne. Tara feels the pale gold glowing inside her as she moves through the room with the curator, who is shaking hands and smiling.

Tara sees a man in the passage. He is standing there in her memory as clear as the bruises on her thighs. A man wearing a white shirt, open at the collar. He is standing there in the glowing champagne light.

He knows her friend the curator. He's from Melbourne, he says. He's a curator too. Ross or Russ he calls himself. Something like that. He's arranging a show that will travel here from Melbourne.

He is smiling, friendly. Too friendly. Tara gets a queer feeling when he looks at her. There's something wrong about him. Something wrong about the way the light catches his face, his body.

The light flickers, but it's not the champagne light in the museum. Where is this flickering light? She tries to remember. She remembers being in the car with the two men. She sees streetlights whizzing past the windows.

Now they enter a low-ceilinged room. Voices in the room rise and fall like a sea. Ross or Russ and the curator sit down across from Tara at a table. The three of them are making toasts, clinking glasses. Ruby liquid flows down her throat. Ruby liquid soaks the table cloth. They are laughing.

Ross or Russ is sitting too close to the curator. He is rubbing his leg against Tara's as he sits too close to her friend, the curator. Tara is feeling the warmth of his leg, the warmth of the wine. The wine has transformed Ross or Russ into someone who she likes. When she is drunk she likes everyone.

Ross or Russ is getting married. He's marrying a rich girl in Melbourne. The rich girl doesn't know that he is gay. He's laughing, drinking, telling them this. The three of them are laughing: poor little rich girl in Melbourne.

Tara is standing in the bathroom watching a woman she sees as herself. This woman is drinking at the table with the two men. This woman is laughing. Everything in her mind is soggy with wine. Everything is slowed down.

Tara tries to imagine what is going through the mind of this woman she sees as herself. As Tara stands in the bathroom, a picture of her mother flashes through her mind. That picture of her mother is a clue. That picture starts a train of thought.

How often Tara has said to her mother: You should let people be who they are! You shouldn't pass judgement! You shouldn't tell others how to live!

This woman she sees as herself is feeling proud: she can take people as she finds them—especially when she is drunk. The woman she sees as herself at that table is not like her mother at all.

Tara tries to focus, but her vision is as blurred as that of the woman who staggers toward the car. The street rolls like waves in the ocean. In the car, nothing is clear except for the hand on her thigh. The hand belonging to Ross or Russ. As Tara remembers, the voices of the two men sound as though they are a million miles away.

"It's so late. Why not stay over?" says the curator to Ross or Russ.

"I'll just see Tara home first," he replies.

Tara stands in the bathroom light while this woman she sees as herself moves through the darkness, held upright by his arms. He carries her through the dark rooms to her bed. She is saying goodnight in a groggy voice when suddenly she feels his body on top of hers. She is pushing against his body. Pushing with all her might. But her eyes are heavy. As heavy as his body. As heavy as this darkness.

Tara has lost this woman in the darkness while she stands in the bathroom light. Tara has lost this woman she saw as herself. This woman has slipped through the hole in her memory. There is only Tara now, standing in the bathroom light with bruises on her thighs, looking for the woman she has lost.

Tara remembers nothing else. She only knows there is a hole in her memory. There is a place inside her where something is missing. Later, she will bury this part of her that is missing. She will bury it with the bruises. She will bury it with the memory of the woman she saw as herself. She will bury it in a place inside her reserved for the darkest corner of Australia.

The Whore

In Trieste, my husband and I, who are traveling,
notice in a dark scruffy bar a middle-aged red-
haired whore with numbers on her arm, sitting at
the next table, smoking. My husband, who is
German, starts a conversation with the woman.
She is from Yugoslavia, she tells my husband in
German. Her skirt is short and tight, raised high
on her thighs. Her eyes are lined with black, her
lips are painted red, her green top fits tight across
her breasts. In no time, my husband and the
woman become engrossed in conversation. The
woman relates gruesome details of her internment
at Buchenwald during the war, which led to her
present profession. I barely understand her
account. English is my native tongue. I don't speak
German well. My husband, spellbound by her tale,
has forgotten my presence. I nudge him, hoping he
will translate what I fail to understand, but he
absently pushes my hand away. I turn my eyes
toward the streaked windowpane, amazed by my
husband's preference. I, who am young, pretty, and
spared by misfortune, feel jealous of this woman
scarred by life.

Marzipan

At a crowded party a pretty girl closes her eyes and bites into a marzipan pear, a look of rapture on her face. "I just love marzipan!" she says to the tipsy young Englishman beside her.

The haughty young man, who seems to be posing, says with a mocking smile, "Balzac loved marzipan too." His bright blue eyes intrigue her. "There was once a rumor in Paris that he opened a candy store just to sell marzipan. But the truth was Balzac always bought marzipan from the same shop." There is a mischievous gleam in his eye. "For a while crowds swarmed to this store to sample the sweet."

"Did you just make that up?" asks the girl, her mouth full.

"It's a true story," the young man replies.

"What a silly story!" laughs the girl, taking another marzipan fruit from the dish on the table. She likes his curly hair, she wonders what's behind his mocking smile. "How do you know such a silly story?" she asks.

"I'm a poet and a food lover," the young man says, half-serious. "When I tire of poetry, I read the food encyclopedia just for fun."

As the girl laughs, licks her sticky fingers, and chooses another marzipan morsel, the poet glances at the other guests. After quickly appraising the girls, he turns back to the one beside him.

"How do you stay so thin?" he asks, as she toys with a marzipan apple.

"Metabolism I guess. I never gain weight," she lies. "What other silly stories can you tell me?" she says, to change the subject.

He pauses for a moment, swaying slightly. His every move seems mannered, artificial; he plays a role, but knows he plays it well.

"I know so many stories," he smiles. "During the blockade of Malta by the English and the Neapolitans, the people had nothing to eat but domestic animals like dogs, cats, rats, and donkeys. In time they came to prefer donkey meat over beef and veal." He raises his brows and waits for her reaction.

"That's an awful tale!" she laughs, as she munches on another piece of marzipan. "Tell me another."

For a moment the poet seems to have lost his memory; his mind goes blank as he stares into the distance. His mocking smile disappears. Suddenly he blurts out, "My mother killed herself in 1978." The girl looks at him, surprised. The man turns a deep shade of pink and lowers his eyes; he wonders what came over him.

"I'm so sorry," says the girl, removing her hand from the candy dish.

"So am I," says the man, who knows he's ruined his performance; he feels the curtain falling on his stage. The scent of the almond-flavored sweet, however, stirs his memory; he suddenly recalls how much his mother loved marzipan. Angry at himself, he avoids the girl's eyes as he thinks about his hours wasted in the library searching for stories to use at parties, where he feels shy, where he rarely meets girls, where he's so afraid someone will see how much he has been hurt. As he turns to walk away, he tosses a piece of marzipan into his mouth, but its taste gives him no pleasure.

Attraction

One evening in an outdoor cafe in Oaxaca, a middle-aged man, with red hair and a bushy mustache, suddenly turns his chair around to face the woman seated at the next table. He places his beer beside her glass. Surprised, she looks at his gaunt face, his heavy-lidded, slightly bulging eyes. He seems to regard her with amusement. "Your first time here?" he asks.

"Yes," she cautiously replies, appraising his terry cloth top that looks like two towels sewn together.

"On vacation?" he asks.

She looks at him again. She nods. What attracts her to this man? she wonders. He seems familiar. She feels as though they've met before. His voice is soft and seductive. No, she doesn't want a beer. Mineral water will be just fine.

"I know every town from here to the border," he says. "I've been living in Mexico for almost twenty years."

"What do you do here?" the woman asks.

He gives her a little smile. "Oh, I get by," he says, dragging on his cigarette. "Sometimes I run out of money. Then I have to return to the States, but I always come back."

She is unimpressed by his reply.

"What do you do?" he asks.

"I'm a writer," she says.

"I could tell you stories that would curl your hair!" he says. "It would take you a lifetime to write all my stories."

Why would she want to write his stories? she says to herself, annoyed. She turns her eyes toward the delicate latticework of the gazebo in the plaza across the street.

He says, "A few years ago when the earthquake struck, I was in the States. But when I offered my help, the embassy paid my flight back."

She looks at him. Does he really expect her to believe that? Does he take her for a fool? Silent, she turns her eyes again toward the plaza and follows jets of water gushing from the fountain. Perhaps he doesn't believe she's a writer: perhaps he thinks she's a liar and a drifter like him.

He moves his face closer to hers as he sees her eyes wander.

Suddenly a blonde girl appears as if out of no-where and throws her arms around his neck. As the writer moves over to allow the blonde to pull up a chair, she watches him kiss the blonde girl's cheek. How can she be jealous of this girl? she wonders.

"We're staying at this fleabag hotel," the blonde says to her, giggling. "Last night he lost the key. At 4 A.M. we had to break the window so he could climb inside and unlock the door. We were drunk.

What a mess! The owner almost called the cops!"

The writer smiles, pretends to be amused. She watches the blonde pay his check. She's not surprised. Growing up, she watched her mother pay her father's bills. He's like her father, she tells herself. No wonder he seems so familiar.

"We heard about this bar that's got some late-night action if you want to come with us," he says to the writer.

"Not tonight. Maybe some other time," she says.

He and the girl rise from the table and say goodnight.

Alone, the writer orders a double shot of whiskey, something she hasn't done for years, while several blocks away at the bar with the blonde, the red-haired man rustles through his pants for loose change.

Apples and Bananas

Ready to leave for work, the young man from Ceylon, employed as a part-time proofreader, wears a smart suit and carries a brand-new attaché case, though there is nothing inside but his sandwich. He is all dressed up to impress the parents of his girlfriend. He will meet them for the first time after work.

Pausing by the hall mirror, he puts the case down to straighten his tie. The deep rich brown of his neck contrasts with his white shirt collar. His eyes, black and bright as polished onyx, study the snapshot of his girlfriend stuck in the edge of the frame; he sees a smiling Filipino girl with saffron skin and long straight hair. Her parents want her to marry a white man. As he thinks about her parents, his anger grows: after all, he is a scholarship student; he gets good grades, he is popular, attractive—even to white girls! He opens the attaché case, takes out the sandwich, decides to leave the case at home.

Hours later, when he walks through the door of his girlfriend's tiny plant-filled studio, her parents' sullen faces hide their shock. He is darker than most black men, they think to themselves. Tension fills the air as the daughter introduces them, then leads him to a chair across from her parents, seated on the couch.

Leaning over the coffee table between them, the parents tell the young man how hard they've worked to send their girl to college. They've had such high hopes for her future, they say. The young man listens until he feels ready to burst. "With or without your consent," he says, his black eyes flashing, "Nicole and I intend to marry!" The couple look down at the rug. The girl looks anxious when she sees a tear roll down her mother's cheek. Impulsively, the young man reaches over and grabs a banana from the fruit bowl on the coffee table. "In my country," he says, excitedly, "Hindu legend claims that the banana—not the apple—was the fruit forbidden to Adam and Eve. But the Hindu version also ends with their expulsion from Paradise: whether Eve ate an apple or a banana the story is essentially the same: it doesn't really matter which fruit was forbidden. Why should it matter if I'm Indian, so long as I love your daughter and she loves me!"

The mother dabs her eyes. "I don't care about apples and bananas, but I care about my daughter," she says, hanging her head. The husband clasps his wife's hand. Resigned, they rise; the girl sees them to the door.

At first the girl feels sad. She had wanted her parents to be as happy as she is. She is still thinking of them when he removes his jacket and loosens his tie. But when he unbuttons her blouse and pulls her skirt over her head, she forgets about her parents. When they are naked, the girl says, coyly, "Too bad we have no fig leaves, or should I say, banana leaves."

Laughing, he takes her in his arms. "This is still Paradise," he says and glances at the hanging plants by the window, which shield them from prying eyes across the street.

Her Room

Her room has a window, small and high, not much more than a slit in the wall with a screen to keep out mosquitoes. A crude wood dresser with a round mirror faces the bed. From the porch, gleaming tin roofs touched by sun can be seen through the trees. Downstairs, the hotel manager, with slick black hair, holds open his greasy palm while a guest fumbles through his pants for pesos. A few miles off in a frothing sea, a party of sun-tanned tourists scuba dive; like a school of strange fish, their fins and snorkels bob in the water. Crimson mingles with turquoise and purple as divers, flung against coral, emerge with bloody legs and feet. Up the coast, tour boats dock near large pools with half-dead turtles; children ride upon their backs. Other pools, once filled with sharks, are empty. On shore, smiling vendors lure tourists inside small stalls filled with blouses and beads. In town, between cafes and boutiques—with mementos priced in dollars—fishermen doze in hammocks in small dim huts furnished with madonnas and TVs. Clouds of sand sail through narrow streets into huts and hotel lobbies while hordes of tourists prowl. Sputtering motorbikes, blaring music, drunken shouts drown out the sound of cicadas at night. Fireflies dance to strange songs. Fishermen, almost barefoot, wearing sandles made of leather thongs and rope, tie weathered boats to the dock. While she lies in her room, eyes closed, the sea roars, foaming, furious at the island tip, whipping the rocks without pity.

The Terrace

Reluctantly, the girl takes a bus from the city to her art dealer's housewarming party in the suburbs. Other guests arrive in taxis, cars, and chauffered limousines. Crumpled gift wrappings clutter the vestibule. The girl, without a present, sheepishly greets the art dealer, who exhibits her paintings at his gallery in the city. "How ingenious!" he remarks, when he learns she took the bus. Outside the sprawling rooms of the penthouse enclosed in glass, a wide overhanging terrace faces the river. Elegant guests wear designer gowns and hairdos as carefully modeled as the sculptures scattered through the house. The girl gazes at porcelain vases and art nouveau glass safely displayed in locked cases. Men with manicured nails, jeweled cuff links, and gleaming smiles seem lifted like cutouts from magazines. Perfumes scent the air. Slim waiters serve champagne and hors d'oeuvres on silver trays. The crowd swells and seems to move en masse toward the terrace. Silk rustles, glasses clink, diamonds flash, and small painted mouths take dainty bites of exotic tidbits.

The girl feels ill at ease. She dreams that the terrace—weighed down by guests—begins to crack:

there are screams and cries; the blue tiled floor heaves and buckles; delicate trunks of young trees break; the terrace crashes thirty floors below. Ladies and gentlemen are thrown to their deaths. Trembling servants rush to assist those who barely escaped disaster: hysterical women are silenced with sedatives, while pale men mop their brows with monogrammed handkerchiefs. The girl helps the servants bring tea to the injured and bandage wounds of those who scrambled to safety Now no one will notice that her dress is not of the finest fabric; no one will gaze with disapproving eyes at her hair that was not arranged by expert hands. Now it doesn't matter whether her shoes have marched through mud or the marble halls of palaces.

Without Shame

There's one mansion after another here. Street after street of rich people, though there's no one in sight. The mansions and the lawns look so perfect it's hard to believe anyone lives here. But he assures me people live in these mansions. People richer than he is. People richer than his family. He is not rich in comparison to the people who live in these mansions. That's why the man who was left for a cook likes to come here. He comes here to feel poor. He feels poor before he comes here, but only when he comes here can he admit to himself he feels poor. Away from these streets, he can't reconcile being rich and feeling poor, so he hides what he is feeling. Away from these streets, he can't understand how his lover could leave him for a cook! He comes here to dull the pain. Here, the man who is rich can feel poor; a poor man can be left for a cook without shame.

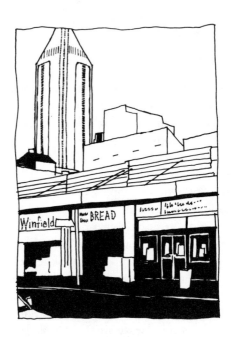

The Mugger

Over drinks at a midtown bar, an attractive well-dressed novelist casually tells his friend, a woman with long stringy hair, "I mugged a man last night."

Her eyes open wide. "You what?" she cries, almost spilling her drink.

"I mugged a man last night," he repeats, in the same dry tone.

"Why?"

"I don't know," he replies. "I felt like it. I took off my shoe and threatened a stranger on the street. It was late at night. The man was old. I told him to give me all his money and he did. About eighty bucks. I stuffed it in my shoe and walked away. I was rather sloshed: I was coming from a party."

"I can't believe it. You've gone mad!" she says, shaking her head. "Eighty bucks? You did it for eighty bucks? Eighty bucks is nothing to you! You spend eighty bucks on lunch—though God knows how you manage on the money you make." The woman, a painter, looks around the room and fidgets with her napkin; she feels out of place in the bar filled with businessmen.

"Don't remind me of my debts," the novelist sighs, stirring his scotch. "I owe my tailor a fortune! It's expensive having wealthy friends."

"But you get invited everywhere," she says. "Think of all the free vacations you've had." She feels a twinge of envy when she thinks about the trip to Turkey she can't afford to take. Crumbling the napkin in her hand, she says, "I don't understand it. Why don't your rich and famous friends help you sell your book?"

The novelist feels his anger rising. He gulps down the rest of his drink. She has large pores, he is thinking. She wouldn't like it if I told her that she has large pores.

"That poor man you mugged!" she continues. "You should have mugged one of your so-called friends at the party."

Silent, the novelist gives her a long hard look, then turns to call the waiter for the bill. The woman searches through her purse for money.

The Beheading

We are driving through the bush in a jeep. I feel free driving through the bush, especially since I'm not driving. He's driving. The one his mother-in-law calls "The Dwarf." She doesn't call him "The Dwarf" because he's short. She calls him "The Dwarf" because his body is much too small for his head. I bet his head weighs half as much as his body, though there's no way to prove that without beheading him, which is not something I'm about to do. But it would be nice and quiet in this jeep if someone here—like his wife for instance—got the urge. His wife would be most likely to behead him since she's the one he's complaining about. Everything she does, or did in the past, gives him cause for complaint. As a nurse, she probably knows the cleanest, most efficient way of beheading him, though that's probably not something they teach in nursing school. If I were a nurse, and knew how to do it, I wouldn't be surprised to see his head flying over the banksia and the scrub and the stunted trees growing here in the bush. Then I could concentrate my attention on the scenery. In the distance there's a sliver of sea.

The Door

Locked out, the Englishwoman, an artist whose hair is dyed deep purple, stands beside her guest in the dark by the door of the secluded country house in the woods. The Englishwoman holds a hatchet in her hands.

"We have no choice but to break down the door," she giggles.

"We'll never get through those windows," her guest says, solemnly shaking her head.

"Poor old door," the Englishwoman moans in a mocking voice.

Back from a hike, the women found a note from a friend who dropped by and locked the door when he found no one home: he didn't know the Englishwoman and her husband only lock the door when they leave for the city. Away on a business trip, her husband took the car and the only set of keys. The house is miles from town.

The guest says, "Your husband thinks of no one but himself."

The couple keep nothing of value in the country house. Although they are rich, the furniture is ratty, secondhand, bought in haste. Clothes lie strewn over every chair. Dirty dishes, unwashed glasses, empty liquor bottles, and magazines clutter the rooms, with unmade beds and soiled mattresses lying on the floors. The lawn is never mowed. Weeds grow waist high. Leaves and insects float on the cloudy surface of the swimming pool. The husband refuses to spend money on this house he rarely visits, though his wife stays here often. In winter a solid sheet of ice covers the driveway, which stops a few feet from the edge of a cliff. But no one clears away the ice. In the city the couple entertain his business friends with lavish parties where the Englishwoman plays the perfect wife.

The guest, also an artist, is very poor. She winces at the thought of smashing the sturdy old door— the door the husband recently paid a carpenter to repair. He had no problem paying the carpenter, but he is stingy with his wife's allowance. She often feels as poor as her guest.

Laughing, the Englishwoman swings the hatchet high in the air.

"Your husband will have a stroke!" the guest says, beginning to laugh as well.

"Yes, I know," the Englishwoman says, laughing even harder.

"I can just see his face!" says the guest, barely able to control herself. Their shrill laughter dulls the sound of splintering wood.

Them

On the island lives a creature that lives nowhere else in the world. It looks like a rat, but it has a pouch like a kangaroo. Everywhere I go I see them. The island is swarming with them. I almost step on one eating a fruit in the grass. The Dutch—who never meant to come here—named the island after them. The Dutch thought they looked like rats too. Tourists from the mainland ooh and aah when their leader points them out. It's odd these tourists need a leader to point them out. What do these tourists see? I wonder. Maybe if they didn't have a leader, they would spot the creatures on their own. They wouldn't be waiting for their leader to do it for them. Once they see the creature they don't seem to notice the peacocks or the deafening noise of the ravens, which sound as though they're gagging. Myself, I prefer the salt lakes—seven times saltier than the sea—and the twisted trees and the tracks overgrown with weeds where the train doesn't run anymore.

Without Fear

That morning as they drove through the desert, the curator pointed out grass trees, some three meters high, some a thousand years old, but the woman couldn't care less. She was tired of the desert, tired of the heat, the empty road, the empty sky. She acted as though nature put this desert here to tire her.

Then suddenly there was a town. Before she knew what happened, there were streets, houses, shops. There was a beach, a quiet bay. Suddenly there was something to see besides the desert. There was something to see, but there wasn't much. There were just enough streets so she knew this was more than a stage set, more than a mirage. But not much more. "This is it?" she asked, looking at him in disbelief. "This town has a regional branch of the museum?" The curator tried to stay calm. He was doing his best to keep from throttling her.

After her lecture—which was well attended despite her conviction that no one would come in this heat—an art student approaches the woman. She is the wife of an engineer. "I really enjoyed your talk," she says. "It's such a treat to have an artist from New York here. How do you like Australia?"

"Not much," the woman replies.

"Maybe you haven't seen the right places," the student says. "I have some time. I could show you around if you're free."

"Sure," she says, with a shrug.

The curator breathes a sigh of relief when he sees her go off with the student.

As they walk toward the beach, the student says, "I have two small children. It's hard to find time for art school. My husband wants me to stay home with the kids."

The woman is about to reply when her attention is diverted by small groups of aborigines cooking their midday meals over open fires on the beach.

The student is pleased to see the woman's interest in the aborigines.

"Before we came here, my husband had a job way up north," she says. "There I found aborigine drawings on the rocks in the desert. Finding those drawings opened up another world for me. That's when I started making art. I feel connected to the aborigines because of their feeling for the land. That's what I love about living here—all this land!"

"But it's so empty!" says the woman, looking out past the town.

The student says, laughing, "You're used to crowds in New York. Of course it's empty to you. But there are very special places here. I could show you one of my special places." She looks at her watch. "Then I have to pick up the kids."

"Sure," the woman says, but she feels less than enthusiastic. She doesn't expect much from a student in a small town.

Two aboriginal men wearing only loose trousers walk past them. The woman from New York meets their eyes.

"Their eyes are so alive!" she says to the student, as they head toward her car.

"No one here understands the aborigines," the student says, sighing. "People complain because they can't hold jobs and live on welfare. They don't understand that the aborigines aren't like us. It's hard for them to adjust."

"I heard that aborigines in the city tear up the floors of their flats to use as firewood in winter," says the woman from New York.

"Our world is alien to them," says the student.

"It's not alien to all of them," the woman from New York says. "I met an aborigine at a party. An aborigine with pale blue eyes. Someone whispered to me that he was only five percent aborigine, but he seemed to be making the most of that five percent. The hosts called him an 'authentic aboriginal novelist.' He's married to a French woman and divides his time between Paris and Perth."

"You won't find aborigines like that around here," says the student. "These aborigines want their land back. A few years before I came, they staged a riot and looted the town. You won't see them playing didjeridoos on the streets like the ones in the city."

As the student starts the car, the woman from New York still sees the aborigines' eyes. Looking in their eyes, she saw something. Something like a spark flying, something like a sliver of life that passed from their eyes into hers. It was scary looking in their eyes. It was scary seeing people so alive. She's not used to seeing life up close. She's not used to being part of it.

Beyond the town, there is a smattering of farmhouses, wheat fields. Here and there, strange trees grow sideways. Trunks curve like backs of bent old men laid low by the weight of the sky. The road curves too. The desert looks like a slow undulating sea.

The woman feels more alive, but feeling more alive isn't always feeling better. Feeling more alive is being present to whatever one is feeling.

This time the desert scares her. The desert is so big, so impersonal, so indifferent to human beings. The desert is alive with a secret life buried under sand. She feels the secrets without knowing how to name them. She doesn't want to name them. She doesn't want to feel that secret life.

As they round a bend, a gutted stone village, abandoned by settlers in the last century, stands like broken monopoly houses in the vastness of the desert. The student points out a ruined church.

"That church is special," she says. "I often go there by myself. It's so peaceful and quiet."

"You're not afraid to be alone here?" asks the woman, looking at her with curiosity.

"Oh no," the student replies.

"I'd always be looking over my shoulder," says the woman. "If you happened to run into some crazy person here, you wouldn't stand a chance."

"It's perfectly safe," the student says. She pauses. "Years ago, a man killed several farmers' wives with a butcher knife while their husbands worked in the fields, but he wasn't from these parts. He was passing through. That's the only crime I ever heard about."

"How would you hear about a crime?" asks the woman, looking round her. "Who's here to report it?"

The student grows impatient. "We don't worry about crime," she says.

A few miles past the church, the student turns off on a narrow track lined with twisted trees. The two women drive in silence.

"This is the place I wanted to show you. It's sacred to the aborigines," she says, as they approach through the trees a solitary mountain of striated rock rising high above a natural pool. Through the foliage the woman sees leaves floating in murky water. She is about to say that the pool looks anything but sacred when she raises her eyes and gets a jolt. Looking at the mountain is like looking in the eyes of the aborigines, but this time she sees without fear. She could swear that the mountain is alive; she could swear that it is vibrating with life.

"We can swim here, but don't put your head in the water," says the student as she disrobes. "People say you'll get meningitis and die if you do."

But the woman isn't worried about meningitis. In fact, nothing could be further from her mind than the fear of meningitis as she undresses and follows the student into the water.

The Litter of Leaves

Headed toward newly excavated ruins in the lowland jungle, two American women, a sculptor and a painter, rest beside the trail. Seated upon the enormous roots of an old ceiba tree, the painter gazes overhead at the high canopy of tropical forest, where a moment ago she glimpsed a band of spider monkeys moving through the trees. The sculptor, seated beside her, leafs through her guidebook, then flings it in the bush. Fuming, she says, "If the museum had bought my sculpture, I would be traveling for a year, not three weeks!"

"There's no use complaining now," says the painter in her mild voice.

Not listening, the sculptor says, angrily, "If that lazy dealer of mine had tried just a little bit harder, the curator would have bought it! All he needed was one last push." She flicks an unfamiliar insect from her arm.

"Maybe it's time you looked for another dealer," the painter says, slightly afraid of the sculptor's anger.

"All dealers are alike," she snaps. "Unless you sell your work for six figures, they don't give a damn. Ten thousand dollars is nothing to them."

The painter glances toward the bush where she hears the rustle of an animal while the sculptor continues to complain.

A sudden earth tremor disrupts their trains of thought. Shocked, they grab each other's hands.

"An earthquake?" the sculptor screams.

"Just a small one. It's over now," the painter says.

Rooted to the spot, the sculptor looks at twisted trunks of massive trees straining toward the sky as though suddenly aware of the strangeness of her surroundings. "Imagine, yakking about the art world in the midst of all this!" she says, disgusted with herself.

The painter leads the way along the trail. Through an opening in the bush, the painter sees vine-covered temples rising in half-cleared forest. But the sculptor, looking down at the trail, sees only the litter of leaves at her feet.

Bar Ecology

PeeWee is wearing his teeth today. His mouth is a black hole without them. His mouth reminds me of Edvard Munch's painting *The Scream*.

"How ya doing?" he says to me, settling into his usual seat at the bar.

"I'm fine. How about you?"

He makes a face and motions for his Canadian Club with Coke on the side. He never touches the Coke.

It's 11:30 A.M. PeeWee is my first customer. Sometimes he waits outside for me to open up. He starts the day with three or four rounds, then returns on his afternoon break. He works seven days a week parking cars.

"So what's going on?" PeeWee asks.

"Nothing much," I reply.

My personal life I keep to myself. I let my customers do the talking. I do the listening. I learned that at bartending school.

PeeWee suddenly points to my glass of water and shakes his head. "Never leave your drink on the bar," he says. "You never know what someone will drop into it. Iris, the night girl, left her drink on the bar one night, and someone drugged it when she wasn't looking. Had to call an ambulance. Was LSD or somethin'. You never can tell who'll walk in here. There's all kinds of nuts in this world."

"I'll remember that," I tell him and take my drink off the bar, even though he is my only customer.

"People get crazy in this place sometimes," he says. "One night when Beth was working, this guy grabbed her. Just reached across the bar and grabbed her. I says to him, 'I'll kill ya if you try that again.' I took him by the shirt. 'She's my daughter!' I says. 'You hear me? I'll tear you apart if you touch her!' You can bet he didn't try that again! Ya gotta watch yourself here."

"I'm careful," I say to him, glancing at the baseball bat behind the bar I hope I'll never have to use.

"Some wacko could walk in at any moment, but you know you can always call me. The garage is only four blocks away. I take care of all the girls here."

"Yes, I know."

PeeWee is ready for his second drink. I pour more Canadian Club.

When I started working here, Greta, the senior bartender, poured a shot to show me how much alcohol to serve the customers. She poured twice the measure I was shown at school. They're like babies, Greta said. They scream and cry if you don't fill their glasses. PeeWee is one of the few who never complains.

94

"Did ya hear about the seventeen-year-old girl who jumped out a fourteen-story window?" Pee-Wee says.

"No."

"She was a friend of mine. Lived right next door to me. Jumped fourteen stories. I liked that girl."

"I thought you lived on the third floor," I say to him.

"I do. She used to live right next door. Then she moved in with this guy. Got hooked on drugs. He was no good. I told her, 'You stay with him, you got trouble!' But she wouldn't listen. Jumped fourteen stories.

"There wasn't any fourteen-story apartment buildings where I grew up. There wasn't any drugs either. These kids are soft. They should grow up the way I did on the lower east side. Then they'd be strong. If ya wanted to eat, ya went out and stole. That's how I ate. In the country it was easier. I learned what to eat by watching the animals eat. If an animal eats it, it's good. If an animal sniffs it and walks away, don't touch it."

"I'll remember that."

"It's true! Did you ever see an animal get sick from eating something in the nature?"

"I haven't seen that many animals eat," I have to confess.

"Well, next time you're in the woods, watch the rabbits, the bears, the chipmunks. They know what's good! I followed an animal once and found the best onions I ever ate. Just pulled 'em out of the ground. Those animals, they're smarter than people. People will eat anything you put in front of their faces, but not animals!

"If I didn't have a wife and children and two grandchildren, I'd go back and live in the woods right now. I don't need nothing I can't find in the nature. All I need is my tent for the rain.

"I got a house upstate. Built it myself. When I'm up there, I disappear in the woods for days at a time. When I come back," he chuckles, "my wife says, 'Oh my God!'—because I'm so dirty. She don't understand that I love that dirt."

PeeWee stares into space, smiling to himself as I pour more Canadian Club. I empty his ashtray and turn on the sink. As I run the water, I see that girl falling, falling through the air.

"Yeah, I gotta go to the country soon," PeeWee sighs. "I gotta fix the plumbing in the house. I got a lot of work to do up there."

"How can you go to the country when you work seven days a week?" I ask.

"Oh—I got time coming to me. Damn boss owes me my vacation time. If I don't take it soon, I could be under that dirt before that house gets fixed. You never can tell how long you got in this world."

"No," I agree.

PeeWee stares into space, but this time he's not smiling. His mouth is moving. He is muttering to himself. He no longer sees me. If I spoke to him now, he wouldn't hear me.

Reality

This is the sort of bar I always imagined in Australia. Here, men look like men, big and brawny. They laugh and shout and curse like men. After a hard day's work, they drink like men too. The machismo of these men makes Mexicans look meek. I don't like this bar.

A rough-looking man turns to question me. "Where you from?" he asks, none too friendly.

"New York," I reply.

"You going back?" he asks.

"Yes," I say.

"You can go back *there* after being *here?*" he says, looking at me in disbelief.

"Yes," I say, trying to smile.

"This is reality!" he says, pounding the bar with his big hairy fist. "Tell me what *you* think reality is!" he challenges, a smirk on his face.

Reality is light-years from this bar, I might have the courage to say if I was big and brawny and male. But if I was big and brawny and male I might feel I belong here. I might look at a woman like me and feel the contempt he is feeling.

The Dangers of Lima

Despite warnings from their guide about the dangers of Lima, two American women hail a cab in front of their hotel. Free from their tour for the afternoon, they are going to explore the old center of the city. As the taxi passes colonial-style mansions in a wealthy suburb, the older woman looks out the window and says, "I doubt Lima's more dangerous than New York—even if there is more crime. I think the guide is overreacting: he's just trying to scare us."

"They do have a curfew," her companion reminds her. "Didn't you hear what he said? There are thieves and pickpockets and murderers and more terrorist bombings than ever before."

Waving her hand, the older woman says, "If you're going to worry, you may as well stay home."

"I don't believe in tempting fate," the young woman says, sorry she agreed to go with her.

When the cab stops in the Plaza de Armas, the older woman, who speaks more Spanish than her companion, pays the fare. The driver, however, looks unhappy with the money she has given him.

"Cincuenta!" he shouts.

"What's wrong?" the young woman asks.

"I don't know," says the older woman. "He's saying 'fifty,' but that's what I paid him. Maybe he thinks women alone are easy prey. Open the door!" she says, amidst his shouts.

The two women, their adrenaline pumping, run from the cab and duck inside the cathedral. In a gloomy chapel once rumored to house Pizarro's bones, the women catch their breath. The small dim room smells musty and damp. Flecks of dust float through the air. Flickering candles cast shadows on the walls. A sound other than their heavy breathing startles them. It's a rustling sound.

"A bat?" the young woman asks.

"Could be," the older woman replies.

The young woman finds a side door that opens onto a hot crowded street jammed with traffic. But as they step out onto the dusty sidewalk, the driver leaps from his cab a few yards away.

"Cincuenta!" he shouts at the women, extending his arms so they cannot pass.

"Si, cincuenta!" the older woman shouts back. She turns to her companion and shrugs.

The driver, his eyes black with rage, shows her the coin that she handed him. *"Cincuenta!"* he roars again.

For a moment she wonders if the coin is counterfeit. Then suddenly she understands. She paid the driver only fifty *centimos,* which is half of one *inti,* as Peruvian currency is called. The ride to the center of Lima couldn't possibly have been that cheap. From her handbag, she pulls out a bank note for fifty *inti,* which the driver grabs. In triumph, he hands her the coin and returns to his cab.

"What happened?" asks the young woman.

The older woman shows her the coin worth fifty *centimos.* She says, "I would have needed a hundred of these coins to pay the right fare!" Frowning, she puts it back in her handbag. "I blame our guide for what happened," she says. "If he hadn't harped on the dangers of Lima, I wouldn't have expected the worst. I would have given the driver a chance to explain. I would never have run away."

Later, when the women meet the guide and the rest of the group within walking distance of the cathedral as planned, they tell him about the cab. He laughs when he learns what the driver charged.

The Hat

"If you were in Kentucky now, you'd never find your way back," says the boy from New Zealand. "All the tents in Kentucky are the same color and they're lined up in straight rows." I'm glad I'm not in Kentucky, but this island in Australia is not my favorite place either. It took me half an hour to locate the showers on this campground. I'm not staying in a tent, but I have to use the same showers. I rented a small cabin, where I spent the afternoon lying on a cot reading the newspapers. Earlier, an Asian man and his wife were laughing at me. In fact, all the Asian tourists I saw this morning registered some response when they saw me in my hat. I was wearing a straw hat, the kind peasants wear in the rice paddies. I never wear hats. I bought it on a whim. It was the only hat sold on the island that fit my small head. I felt like someone else wearing my hat. I felt good feeling like someone else—until the Asians saw me. To the Asians I felt like saying: this is not who I am! But I didn't say anything. I came back to my cabin to read the newspapers.

Her Hair

I wonder if it has anything to do with her hair. She wears her hair in a tribal style. I've seen this style in anthropological films and journals. Her hair is parted in three concentric furrows that circle her head. Her head reminds me of freshly mowed fields, though nothing I know grows quite so purple. The hair is purple. Maybe more magenta than purple. I wonder if she wore her hair this way when she was a chemist. I wonder if she had trouble finding work as a chemist. Perhaps she hasn't always worn her hair this way. Since she quit chemistry to become an art historian she can't find a job. She'd like to work at the museum here. She's told me so several times. She would even take a job in another city, though that would mean leaving her husband. For two years since she took her degrees she's been looking for a job. Would anybody tell her if her hair is a problem? Would some museum person tactfully say that her hairstyle would be more appropriate in the jungles of New Guinea than in a stuffy museum in Australia? If no one tells her, will she ever figure it out? Would she change her hairstyle if she knew she would find work?

Perhaps she wouldn't find work even if she changed her hair. Who can answer these questions? Who can tell what will happen in this world?

Certain People

There are certain people who want to make it big. Nothing less will do for them. Nothing less will be enough. They sleep and wake and eat their careers. They fuck and drink and talk their careers. In between they do their work. Even in Western Australia there are people like this. Even here in this city cut off from the world. But a person in Western Australia who feels this way will not stay long in this city.

The bald man's ambitions are too big for the west. He only shows his paintings in the east. He wouldn't demean himself by showing his paintings in Western Australia, except at the museum.

The curator is less than enthusiastic about the bald man's paintings, but he allows himself to be entertained at the bald man's house. The bald man always has plenty of booze on hand. The booze, however, has not clouded the curator's judgement. He knows what he likes. He knows what he likes no matter how much he has to drink.

The bald man is charming. He is a perfect host. He wears Italian designer suits and he lives in an expensive house. He sells his paintings at expensive prices. But he hasn't sold them well enough yet to do without his wife's money.

The head of the art school has a wife, but she does-n't have money. The head of the art school is a sad man, a man who gave up his painting. Now he is only an administrator. He looks like a mole. Every day he burrows through the corridors of academia knowing that he is only an administrator since he gave up his painting.

Something must have happened to this mole-like man, who is the bald man's buddy. Something must have happened to make him give up paint-ing. But he doesn't talk about what happened, not even to his wife.

His wife laughs and says she hardly knows him. His wife is half Indonesian. She is beautiful. The woman from New York wonders how such a beauti-ful woman could marry this mole-like man.

The bald man and the mole-like man have nothing in common with the man whose lover left him for a cook. The man whose lover left him is a business-man. He feels uneasy with people in the arts. If not for the woman from New York—the only artist that he knows—he would never have met the bald man, the mole-like man, or their wives.

But here he is sitting at a table in an outdoor restaurant with the two couples and the woman from New York. The man who was left for a cook looks bored while the woman from New York talks about the art world with the bald man.

The bald man makes some caustic comments about the curator, who hasn't bought his paintings, but his eyes light up when he talks about New York. He knows that one day he will live in New York.

The woman from New York agrees with the curator when it comes to the bald man's paintings. But the bald man has electricity on his side. He is an electric person. Sparks fly from him. He is one of those people who holds your attention because he is lit up inside like a Christmas tree. He could almost light up a city.

The woman from New York is drawn to the bald man's energy, even though she doesn't like his paintings. She is talking to the bald man because she feels drawn to that energy. She is talking to the bald man even though she feels guilty. She feels guilty because she is ignoring the man who was left for a cook while she talks about the art world with the bald man.

The man who was left for a cook would like to talk about something important. Something *he* knows about. He knows about many things, but the art world is not one of them. For example, he knows about history and politics, literature and music. But no one at this table cares about the things he knows. What is he doing here with the woman from New York? What is he doing here with the bald man?

The man who was left for a cook is listening to the mole-like man's wife talk about crafts. She is head of crafts at the art school.

"It's so frustrating," she says. "The painting and sculpture departments won't take crafts seriously. They don't consider crafts to be art. To them, crafts are just something women do. They refuse to see pottery as a form of sculpture. They can't see Indonesian textiles as art."

The man who was left for a cook doesn't know very much about crafts, but he knows about quality.

"I think quality can be the only criterion," he says.

He thinks he knows quality when he sees it. He knows it takes time and patience and skill to make something of quality. He knows it takes time and patience and skill to get something just right. Sometimes one never gets it right. Sometimes it falls apart in one's hands no matter how hard one tries. Is making a pot so different from shaping one's life?

Since his lover left him he's been thinking about his life. His life looks like pieces of a shattered pot. But he wouldn't be thinking about his life right now, he wouldn't be thinking about pots, if he were having a quality conversation.

The woman from New York is glad to see that he is talking. She feels less guilty when she sees that he is talking. He looks more at ease when he is talking, even though this isn't the quality conversation that he wants.

While he is talking, he is feeling angry at himself. He is angry at himself for being weak. If he were strong, he wouldn't have allowed the woman from New York to bring him to this dinner. If he were strong, he would be home now in the house where his lover left him. There he could be doing something useful: he could be reading history or philosophy: he could be trying to make sense of his life. He could be trying to figure out what went wrong. Instead, he is here at this dinner talking to the half Indonesian woman so he doesn't have to listen to the bald man.

He had hoped that knowing the woman from New York would broaden his outlook, stimulate his mind, help him to understand his pain. But chitchat about the New York art world has nothing to do with his mind or his outlook or his pain. He resents the bald man. He resents the bald man for acting important, for acting as though he's the only one who counts. The bald man is shallow and pretentious, he tells himself.

Even this woman from New York is not what he hoped she would be. Sitting here talking with the bald man, she seems as shallow as the others. As shallow as all the people in this city. Will anyone ever satisfy his expectations?

He remembers the lover who left him. He feels the pain.

He is not the only one who has ever felt pain. Everyone here has felt pain at one time or another. One can see that the mole-like man is feeling pain right now. One can look in his face and see the pain.

Despite the electric sparks shooting out all around him, one has only to look at the bald man to see that he's had pain. Everyone knows the bald man lost all his hair because he worries so much about his career. It takes a lot of worry to lose so much hair. He used to have thick black hair. He used to have a beard. Now there's not a hair left on his face or his body. The doctor said it was worry that caused his disease.

It is unlikely that the bald man will ever have a lover who will leave him for a cook. Women don't leave the bald man. Women are drawn to the bald man. But he only wants the ones who can help his career. His wife does everything for him except hold his brush while he paints. She is smart enough to be indispensable. But still she is not smart enough. A few months from now the bald man will leave her. He will leave her for a woman in public relations in New York. Who can help his career more than a woman in public relations?

Right now he is sitting beside his devoted wife talking to the woman from New York. He is pumping her for information.

"It's been six months," he says, "since I've been to New York. In six months a lot can change in the art world."

He is trying to find out everything she knows. Every piece of gossip. Every sign of changing trends.

He is getting ready to make a move he doesn't know about yet. Even if he knows about this move it's too soon to tell himself. He's not ready to know yet. He's only in the stage of gathering information.

The man who was left for a cook doesn't belong here. He doesn't belong at a table with the bald man. He doesn't interest the bald man, so the bald man doesn't see him. No one likes to sit at a dinner and not be seen.

The woman from New York is sorry she invited him. She should have known better. She should have known he wouldn't like the bald man. But she had a picture of this dinner in her mind before she came. She had a picture of a pleasant dinner. She pictured what she wanted to see. That's how it will happen, she told herself, because she pictured it that way.

Even when her pictures are wrong she is reluctant to give them up. She has trouble seeing people apart from the pictures she makes of them.

The woman from New York feels the sparks flying from the bald man. It's the sparks that keep her talking to the bald man, even though she knows she's being used. Even though she knows he's pumping her for information. It's the sparks that make her forget the man who was left for a cook. The sparks are like firecrackers. The firecrackers keep the woman talking to the bald man. It is exciting to talk to a man who explodes like firecrackers. She is watching his display.

It is less exciting to talk to a man whose lover left him for a cook. Not because he was left for a cook but because he sees himself as a man who was left for a cook. That fact colors his existence. That fact *is* his existence. He was a man who was left for a cook long before his lover left him. His life was traveling on that path long before he met his lover.

The man who was left for a cook isn't thinking about crafts. He is thinking about quality.

"So few people care about quality," he says to the mole-like man's wife. "I used to think artists cared about quality. I used to think artists were different. But now I'm not so sure." As he speaks, he glances at the bald man.

The wife of the mole-like man looks at him quizzically.

The bald man's wife is listening to her husband pump the woman from New York about the art world. She always listens to her husband. But she's not listening hard enough. She's not seeing the signs. She's too close to him to see the signs. She's so close to him she doesn't see where he ends and she begins. She doesn't see herself as someone who begins at a certain place in her own right. She is a role: wife and mother. She isn't playing a role. Playing a role implies there is a person playing it. But she has never looked inside to see that person.

The mole-like man is staring into space. If someone asked him, he wouldn't be able to say what he is seeing. Perhaps he is staring into space in order to see nothing. Perhaps he just wants to see and feel and hear nothing. But it wouldn't be true to say that his mind is blank—his mind isn't blank, it's clouded. He's drawn the shades down over his mind. With the shades down, he's not aware of his thoughts or his feelings. Perhaps he is staring into space so he won't be aware.

The woman from New York is feeling guilty because she isn't talking to the man who was left for a cook. She is being seduced by the bald man. She is being seduced by his electric eyes and the sparks flying all around him. She is being seduced even though she doesn't like him. She doesn't even like the energy he's giving off. She's just drawn to it.

In truth, she prefers the man who was left for a cook. She can see he is a man of quality—a man with high moral values. Someone else might see that, like the bald man, his eyes focus only on himself. He is focused only on himself but he can't see. He is filled with moral outrage: how could he—a man of quality—be left for a cook!

Because of his pain he is trying to search inside himself. But he only gives himself a tiny space to search. He is scrambling around inside that tiny space trying to find an end to the pain.

The bald man is trying to extend himself into the world. He is trying to fill the world with his presence. He doesn't look inward. He lets his brush do the looking. He lets his brush tell the canvas what he's found. The brush lets out the world inside him. He only sees what his brush has found.

The man who was left for a cook is trying to look inward, but he doesn't have a mirror to see himself. He doesn't see an end to the pain. He needs someone to guide him inside. But he's too proud to ask for help. He's too proud to show his weakness.

He is hiding himself from others while he tries to look inward. He wants no one to see what's inside, at least until he's seen it himself. Right now he doesn't know what can be seen of him.

In his way he is trying to find out what he doesn't see. Because he doesn't see, he is like a blind man bashing his head against the walls. But that is showing him his limits. That is showing him how much he doesn't see. Even his pain has limits. He is looking for a door behind the pain. He is looking for his door. Even in a very small space there is a door. His hands are fumbling along the walls for that door. If only he could find that door, he could step out into the world and he could let himself be part of it despite people like the bald man, the mole-like man, and the woman from New York.

COLOPHON

Certain People was designed by
Christopher Fischbach and Allan
Kornblum, using Adobe Garamond and
Tekton typefaces. Coffee House books are
printed on acid-free paper, and are smyth
sewn for reading comfort
and durability